BORIS AND BELLA

WRITTEN BY **CAROLYN CRIMI**

ILLUSTRATED BY **GRIS GRIMLY**

Harcourt, Inc.

Orlando Austin New York San Diego Toronto London

www.HarcourtBooks.com

Library of Congress Cataloging-in-Publication Data
Crimi, Carolyn.
Boris and Bella/Carolyn Crimi; illustrated by Gris Grimly.
p.   cm.
Summary: Bella Legrossi and Boris Kleanitoff, the messiest and cleanest monsters
in Booville respectively, do nothing but argue until the
night of Harry Beastie's Halloween party.
[1. Monsters—Fiction.   2. Cleanliness—Fiction.   3. Friendship—Fiction.
4. Halloween—Fiction.]
I. Grimly, Gris, ill.   II. Title.
PZ7.C86928Bo   2004
[E]—dc21   2003007478
ISBN 0-15-202528-6

C E G H F D

Printed in Singapore

The illustrations in this book were done in black ink
and watercolor on coldpress watercolor paper.
The display type was set in House of Death.
The text type was set in Throhand Ink.
Color separations by Colourscan Co. Pte. Ltd., Singapore
Printed and bound by Tien Wah Press, Singapore
This book was printed on totally chlorine-free Stora Enso Matte paper.
Production supervision by Sandra Grebenar and Ginger Boyer
Designed by Lydia D'moch

Bella Legrossi was the messiest monster in Booville.
Her slime was the slimiest; her grime was the grimiest.
Her piles of lizard gizzards blocked the doorways,
and her stacks of snake tails overflowed her counters.
None of the other monsters could stand Bella's mess,
so Bella lived by herself.

Boris Kleanitoff was the tidiest monster in Booville.
He vacuumed his vampire bats, dusted his spiderwebs,
and polished his pythons daily. No one could stand Boris's
persnickety ways, so Boris lived alone.

Bella and Boris were neighbors. They did not get along.

"Clean up those crusty old cauldrons! I'm sick of your cluttered yard!" Boris would shout.

"Can't you stop those bewitched broomsticks from sweeping? They're driving me batty!" Bella shouted back.

And so it went, day in and day out.

When Bella had a bar-boo-cue, she did not invite Boris.

And on Valentine's Day, Boris sent chocolate-covered gargoyle boils to everyone but Bella.

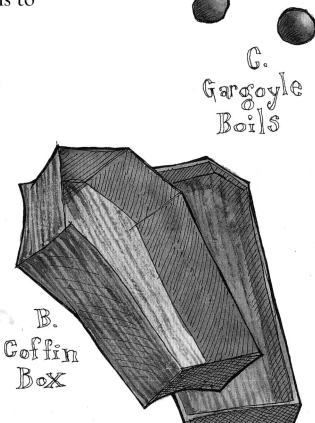

C.
Gargoyle
Boils

Goat guts are red.
Rat tails are pink.
Bella's a drip,
and her feet really stink.

A.
Poem

B.
Coffin
Box

Then came Halloween.

"I think I'll have a Halloween party," said Bella. She made a long guest list, with everyone on it but Boris.

When Boris heard about Bella's party, he decided to have his own. *Who needs Bella's stupid shindig?* he thought. He invited everyone but Bella.

Both monsters mailed their invitations, and both waited for the replies.

"I'm not coming to your party,"
Frank Stein said to Bella.
"Why not?" Bella shouted.
"I'm going to Harry Beastie's party. His dust bunnies
don't bite, and he makes great caterpillar cupcakes."
Monsters called Bella for the rest of the day.
Everyone was going to Harry Beastie's
party instead of hers.

Meanwhile, more monsters called
Boris about *his* party.

"I can't come to your party," said Morrie Mummy.

"Why not?" Boris demanded.

"I'll be at Harry Beastie's party. He doesn't worry
about claw marks scuffing the floors."

Halloween night soared in on bat wings.
It was cold and dark, the perfect night for a party.

Bella sat by herself in her messy cave. "Drat that Harry Beastie! My party would have been an absolute scream!"

Boris sat by himself in his tidy dungeon. "Drat that Harry Beastie! My party would have been frightfully delightful!"

Bella stomped out of her cave. She was going to give Harry a piece of her mind.

Boris stormed out of his dungeon. How dare that Harry Beastie ruin everything!

"Out of my way!" yelled Bella. She pushed Boris aside and tromped into the party, tracking mud all over.

"You get out of *my* way!" demanded Boris. He pushed Bella back and wiped his feet on the mat.

The guests couldn't hear them. They were too busy shrieking and screeching.

"Humph!"
said Bella.

"Humph!"
said Boris.

Bella and Boris wandered over to the boo-ffet. Bella sniffed the snake-spit stew. "Not as slobbery as mine," she said.

Boris nibbled a maggot muffin. "Too much muffin — not enough maggot," he mumbled.

Bella watched some monsters play Pin the Head on the Headless Horseman. "What a bore," she sneered.

Boris eyed the monsters bobbing for eyeballs. "What a snore," he said.

Just then the Howling Wolfman Band burst into the monster mambo. Soon every ghoul in town was shaking and quaking. Cy Clops bebopped and the Fang flip-flopped. The Boogeyman boogied while the trolls twirled round. Baggo Bones connected his hipbones to his neckbone just for fun. Morrie Mummy was swinging so hard he came undone.

"Look at them carrying on," Bella mumbled.

"They're making fools of themselves," Boris said.

The music played on while the two monsters watched everyone else have a good time.

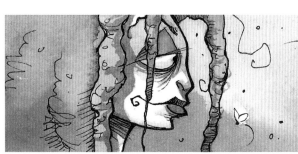

Bella sighed. She loved to dance.

Boris looked down at the floor. He hadn't danced in so long.

Bella looked at Boris shyly. "Maybe we should show them how it's done," she said.

Boris smiled. "We could try," he said.

When Bella and Boris came together, they discovered an amazing thing.

"You're just the right size!" they cried.

The two monsters galumphed
and galomphed in perfect time to
the music. They danced so well,
the other monsters cleared off the
dance floor to watch.

"Not bad for a grime fighter
like you!" said Bella.

"And you're pretty good for
the queen of unclean!" said Boris.

After their dance, they shared a bubbly cup of ghoul drool. When Bella wiped her mouth on her sleeve, Boris didn't say a word. And when Boris cleaned his cup with his handkerchief, Bella didn't tease him.

At midnight, everyone lifted their cups and roared. In the corner of the room were the two new friends, grinning at each other with their snaggletoothed smiles.

"Happy Halloween, Boris Kleanitoff!"

"Happy Halloween to you, Bella Legrossi!"

From that night on, Bella tried to be a little tidier. Boris tried to be a little messier. And when Halloween rolled around the next year, they threw the best bash Booville had ever seen...

. . . together.